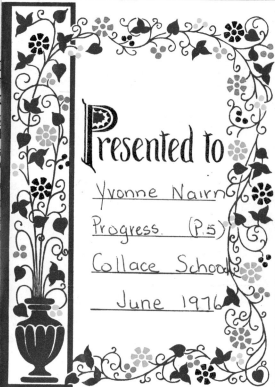

Presented to

Yvonne Nairn

Progress. (P.5)

Collace School

June 1976

PICKERING & INGLIS LTD.   PRINTED IN GREAT BRITAIN

Ellen
and the Queen

GILLIAN AVERY

with illustrations by Krystyna Turska

COLLINS · LIONS

First published 1971 by Hamish Hamilton Children's Books Ltd
First published in Lions 1975
by William Collins Sons and Co Ltd
14 St James's Place, London SW1

© 1971 Gillian Avery
© Illustrations 1971 Krystyna Turska
Printed in Great Britain
by William Collins Sons and Co Ltd Glasgow

CONDITIONS OF SALE
This book is sold subject to the condition
that it shall not, by way of trade or otherwise,
be lent, re-sold, hired out or otherwise circulated
without the publisher's prior consent in any form of
binding or cover other than that in which it is
published and without a similar condition
including this condition being imposed
on the subsequent purchaser

THE chattering children jigged up and down, or craned forward to peer up the road. Over their heads flapped the banner that Miss Higgs, the schoolmistress, had helped them make. 'Welcome to Winterbourne,' it said in white tape tacked on to red calico, and 'Long Life to his Lordship and her Ladyship.'

'They're coming, they're coming!' shrilled the children. 'I can hear the wheels! I can hear 'em shouting back in the village!'

'Stand still then,' ordered Miss Higgs, 'until the carriages reach us. Then girls, remember your curtseys, and boys, your hats.'

But they couldn't stand still. The Earl
and the Countess were coming back to
Winterbourne, to live at the Great
House. None of them could remember

2

The Family living there, for the Old Earl had gone away to live in foreign parts before any of them were born, and the Great House had stayed empty and shut up in its huge parklands beyond the village. But now, in the spring of 1853, the New Earl, his son, was coming to live there, and things would be as they were in the old days, their parents told them, with The Family taking an interest in the village. Maybe the villagers would even be asked up to the Great House, which none of the children had ever seen, for special festivities. Above all, they wanted to see a real lord. What was the use of Winterbourne belonging to an earl if they never saw him?

'Will there be lots of carriages? How will we know which one the Earl's in? Will we see the young ladies and gentle-

men too? Will they be wearing silks and
satins?'

Only Ellen Timms, nine years old,

with fiery red hair and a fiery temper to
match it, stood morosely apart from the
chattering excitement. She had not

wanted to be there at all. She had wanted to be at the Lodge with her mother, opening the gates so that the Earl's carriages could pass within the great grey walls of the park, and drive up the long avenue. But her mother, to her surprise, had no intention of allowing this, and Ellen had been sent to school, like anybody else.

'Now then, children,' said Miss Higgs, 'step forward. And when I say "one, two, three", start singing.'

The leading carriage in the procession drew to a halt opposite the little school, and the girls dropped curtseys and the boys pulled off their hats and knuckled their foreheads. But then they were so overcome at the magnificence of the carriages that they could only stare at the glossy paint, the coats of arms on the doors, the gleaming horses in their silver harness, and the men who drove them, splendid in dark green with silver buttons, and cockaded hats.

'One, two, three,' said Miss Higgs, but only one or two quavering voices joined in the song she had specially made up and taught them for the occasion.

> *Our Earl we greet,*
> *Oh may his feet*
> *Long walk his native places.*
>
> *Oh see us stand*
> *With upraised hand*
> *And happy eager faces.*

At the words 'upraised hand' they were all supposed to fling up their own hands and round off the song with three cheers, but they completely forgot this, and Lucy Baines had to have a little push from Miss Higgs before she tottered forward on legs stiff with fright to thrust a garland of primroses at the window of the front carriage.

'For her ladyship,' she gabbled. But she only remembered because Miss Higgs was whispering it in the background.

A window glass was lowered, somebody put his head out and thanked them, and then with a great clattering of hooves and crunching of wheels the carriages moved off again. Miss Higgs went into the school-house and the children came alive again, and their tongues were unloosed.

'Was that his lordship? Him as looked out?'

'Lor, Luce, I thought you was going to poke off his nose with them flowers!'

'Did you see the young ladies? There was one as young as us in the carriage at the back, and two or three that were littler.'

'Lor, didn't Miss Higgs' voice sound wobbling, didn't it just!'

'I don't wonder,' said Ellen savagely, 'with all those silly words.'

They all stopped their chatter and stared at her. 'Ellen Timms, you didn't ought to speak like that. It rhymed a fair treat; you try and do better. You couldn't, could you?'

Then Sarah Jarvis, sharper than the rest, scored a hit. 'Don't you take no notice of her talk. She's real cross, the nasty jealous thing, because she said she'd be at the Lodge opening the gates, and now she isn't.'

There was enough truth in this to send Ellen into one of her famous rages. The Timms family had only been at the Lodge for a week, but everybody had had enough of Ellen's boastings. Every day they heard about how Mr Sowerby, the Earl's agent, had come to Mrs Timms' cottage in the village ('and taken off his hat. Just fancy, Mr Sowerby taking off his hat to our Mam!') and told her that the Earl had written to ask Mrs Timms and her 18-year-old son Joe to be the new lodge-keepers. They had heard of the glories of the Lodge, the porch with pillars and the brass knocker with a lion's head (but anybody who passed the gates of the Great House could see this for themselves). They heard about the parlour, and the kitchen with a proper cooking stove. But most of all they heard about how Ellen was going to be there opening the gates when The Family came back. More than that, there was talk of the Queen herself coming to pay a visit to the Great House, and who but Ellen would open the gates then!

'Nobody can believe what Carrotty Timms says,' taunted Sarah Jarvis. It was always good sport to see how angry you could make Ellen.

Ellen pulled off her bonnet and lashed out with it at her tormentors. But there came a sharp rapping on the diamond-paned window of the little school-house; Miss Higgs was watching.

'If you don't watch out, Ellen,' warned Eliza Moon, 'you won't get that special bun Miss Higgs said her Ladyship was sending down to us.'

'Will her Ladyship be bringing them herself?' asked little Lucy Baines.

'Don't be such a little silly,' Ellen told her. 'She's much too grand for that. She just sits still all day.'

Lucy was downcast. 'Won't us ever
see her then?'

'I daresay The Family'll be in church
on Sunday,' said Eliza Moon.

'But we'll only be able to see their tops then,' lamented Lucy.

'What do you mean, Luce?' asked her sister, Mary Ann. 'You can see what they're wearing, and their faces and all.'

'But,' said Lucy, 'I wanted to see . . .' And she stopped.

'What did you want to see, Luce?' encouraged Eliza, who was a motherly sort of girl.

'I wanted to see about their legs,' said Lucy with a rush.

There was a scandalized cry from the knot of girls. 'Legs, Lucy Baines? Better not let Miss Higgs hear you talk like that.'

'Well, ladies haven't got none, have they?' whispered Lucy, scarlet-faced at her own boldness. 'And what I did wonder was when they dropped off.'

'Drop off?' they all echoed.

'Everybody has legs,' said Ellen in a withering manner. 'Unless they are cut off them.'

But Lucy stuck gamely to her point. 'Not fine ladies. They has skirts. Because it's rude to have legs.'

'Well, of all the little sillies,' said Ellen scornfully. 'I thought you was a poor silly thing, Lucy, but not as bad as that.'

In the ordinary way the other children might have told Lucy much the same, but now they all wanted to take sides against Ellen.

'Don't you take no notice, Luce,' comforted Mary Ann. 'There's nobody sillier than Carroty Timms herself — we all knows that.'

'If they haven't got legs, how do you

reckon they move then?' shouted Ellen, fast working herself up into another rage.

'Perhaps it's wheels,' said Lucy between sobs. 'Perhaps they don't drop off, perhaps ladies has them cut off when they get old enough to wear long skirts – like lambs' tails get cut off.'

'Lambs' tails!' repeated Ellen scornfully. 'You're a silly baby, and a cry-baby too.'

'Don't you say such things to her,' said Mary Ann, putting her arms protectingly round her little sister.

'I will then, because it's true, and all of you know it's true, and I'll fight anybody as says it isn't.'

'You prove it then,' shouted Sarah Jarvis tauntingly.

'All right, I will then. Because *I'll* be able to see all the gentry, living at the

16

Lodge. Every day I'll see them, not like you.'

But a few weeks later Ellen had seen no more of the gentry than anybody else. Carriages came and went through the gates by the Lodge, but her mother wouldn't have Ellen opening them. Nor could you see much through the window glass. She saw glimpses of them in church, but the Great House pew in Winter-bourne church was like a separate room. The crimson cushioned seats faced the Rector in his pulpit; there was a separate entrance from the churchyard, and even crimson velvet curtains that could shut off The Family from the rest of the con-gregation.

'You'd only be getting us into trouble. Just look at you now, no bonnet and them red curls all over the place.'

Nor was she allowed to set foot on the other side of the gates, to walk up the avenue and peep at the Great House.

'The Earl wouldn't like it,' her brother Joe told her kindly. 'It would get Mam into trouble, and you don't want us turned away from the Lodge, do you now? Your time will come; they'll be having the village up to the Great House soon, I daresay – perhaps when the Queen comes.'

That was another sore point with Ellen. The Queen was coming, she really was, with Prince Albert and four of their children, to spend a night at the Great House. The Earl was so grand and his house so big that he could do things like this. The village was very proud of him, and they pitied other places that had only a plain 'Mr' or just a 'Sir' for a landlord, and were scornful about 'great houses' that were too poverty-struck for the Queen to visit. There were tremendous preparations going on at their own Great House, and the fathers of many of the children at school were working up there, building, painting, getting the gardens into shape. So every day the girls in Ellen's class could contribute a new wonder their fathers had told them – while Ellen had nothing at all to tell.

Joe worked in the Great House stables, but he had nothing much of interest to tell about that, and Ellen didn't even see the wagons of workmen and materials from Salisbury passing through her gates, because these used a separate entrance.

'Never mind,' Joe comforted her when she complained loudly. 'You'll be seeing it soon, I daresay. There's talk of them putting up tents in the park when the Queen comes, and giving us all tea there.'

But so far as Ellen was concerned, the Countess and Miss Higgs decided other-wise. It happened like this.

It was on a May morning when every-thing was bright and shining outside, and she was aching all over with having to sit still at school. She was supposed to be writing her copies at the long desk under the window while other children were called up to Miss Higgs' table to read. The babies were gabbling their alphabet, first forwards, then backwards, over and over again, and everybody was busy except Ellen. She had written 'Procrastination is the thief of time' four times, each time worse than the one above, and had no wish to write it a fifth. So she poked Eliza Moon with her elbow.

'Why do you write with your tongue sticking out? Our old cat does that if you tickle behind his ears. Shall I tickle behind your ears?'

But Eliza wrote steadily on.

'Or I'll ink your tongue if you like, so's you can write with it.' Ellen jabbed her pen into the ink pot, dragged it out full and pointed it at Eliza, who gave a bleat and jerked herself away.

'Who is that making a disturbance
down there? Ellen Timms. I thought so.
Come out to the front with your copy-
book.' Miss Higgs took out her ruler

meaningly, and laid it in front of her.

Everybody watched while Ellen went up. The babies, still gabbling ZYXW V, stared at her with huge round eyes; the writers held their pens poised over their copies; the group round Miss Higgs' table, clutching their books, fell back to let her pass.

'Disgusting, as I thought,' said Miss Higgs, glancing at the copy, in which 'procrastination' had been spelt four different ways, and which was lavishly spattered with blots. Then Miss Higgs produced the label 'Empty vessels make the most sound' – it was worn by Ellen more than by anybody else in the school – and pinned it to her back.

But Ellen scarcely noticed this time, for she was staring out of the window behind Miss Higgs' back. There was a

carriage drawing up outside the school,
and a man in splendid dark green livery
had jumped down to open the door.

'Get up on the stool, Ellen,' commanded Miss Higgs.

'Oh but . . .' began Ellen.

'Ellen Timms, do as I say at once,' said Miss Higgs scandalized.

But just as Ellen had climbed on to the stool in the corner, the schoolroom door opened and the Countess swept in.

They all scrambled to their feet and stood staring. They had never seen her so close before. She was so big. She was not only tall, but broad; not just comfortably fat like most of their mothers, but all tightly bound up like the staves of a barrel. As she sailed down the room she seemed to dwarf everything in it. And in her wake, like a duckling behind a barge, followed a little girl of about seven, in a tartan dress with a little tartan cape and a green silk bonnet.

'Miss Higgs, I presume?' said the Countess. 'I am sorry that I have not been able to pay an earlier visit to this school which our family founded. The Earl and I propose to take a keen interest in it. I have brought my daughter,

Lady Mary, so that she also may see the children.'

'Your ladyship,' said Miss Higgs, hurrying forward, confused, 'if I had known . . .'

The Countess waved a large gloved hand, and Miss Higgs sank into silence. She looked about her. 'Nice neat hair, I am glad to see. Though one or two of your children could do with tighter braids. I see curls here and there, and curls are things that I will not countenance in my servants, nor at our school. Perhaps you will rectify the matter before my next visit.'

Miss Higgs swallowed and twisted her hands nervously. 'Oh yes, your ladyship, certainly, your ladyship.'

'They are all good children, I hope?' The Countess scrutinized them again.

'And they know their Catechism? Well then, I am going to tell them of a great treat. Her Majesty the Queen . . .' Here the Countess paused impressively. 'Her Majesty the Queen has graciously consented to pass a night at the Great House — as many of you may know. And the Earl and I thought that if the children had been good children — but only on that condition mind — they should come up to the main entrance of the house to see her alight from her carriage.'

There was an excited murmuring among the children, and Miss Higgs stepped forward. 'I am sure we all thank his lordship and her ladyship for their kind thought for the school, don't we, children?'

The Countess waved her hand once more as if to dismiss further talk. Her

eye roved round the schoolroom, and then fell on Ellen for the first time. She pointed an awful finger at her.

'And why, may I ask, is that child there?' She held a pair of glasses up to her eyes. 'She has the most unruly hair I have ever seen on a child. She cannot help its colour, but those curls can, and must be, controlled.'

'Ellen Timms, do you hear what her ladyship says? You had better get down and show her your label.' Miss Higgs unpinned it, put it into Ellen's hands, and gave her a little push forward.

' "Empty vessels make the most sound," ' read out the Countess. 'You have been talking in class?'

Ellen hung her head.

'You see, Mary, what becomes of naughty children in this school,' re-

31

marked the Countess to the little girl at her side.

'Yes, mamma.'

Through lowered eyelashes Ellen looked at the little girl. And she noticed that under the green silk bonnet came hair like her own. It was certainly very smooth, and it was not so bright, but it was red. At the same time she saw the little girl staring back at her – and she seemed to be the one sympathetic person in the room.

When the huge bulk of the Countess had made its stately departure, Miss Higgs told Ellen how she had disgraced the school. 'And of course,' she finished, 'I cannot dream of allowing you to go up to the Great House with the school. Her ladyship said "good children only".'

'Who was going to see ever so much of The Family – more than any of us?' they taunted her in the playground afterwards. 'And now she's not even going to be allowed in the park!'

'I wouldn't be going with you for anything,' said Ellen loftily. 'Going two by two with Miss Higgs! *I* shall be going by myself.'

Little Lucy Baines took no part in any of this back-chat. 'She *was* on wheels – her ladyship – under all them skirts,' she said dreamily. 'She just rolled along so smooth.'

Ellen told the schoolchildren so many times in the next few weeks of how she was going to see the Queen, that in the end she came to believe it herself.

She needed to console herself somehow, after all, for the talk now at school and up and down the village was of nothing but the Queen. The children were practising their curtseys, and learning all the verses of 'God Save the Queen', and stitching at the banners that were to festoon the village street, and wondering which of the little princes and princesses would be coming and what they would be wearing. The village women were scouring and burnishing their cottages. 'You never know, her carriage might just break down outside, and I'd never get over the shame of it if everything weren't just apple-pie order in here,' they told each other. They were trimming up their bonnets too, with every bit of finery they could lay hands on, for on the evening of the Queen's visit there was to be roast beef and plum pudding served in tents in the park to everybody in the village who chose to come.

'It's going to rain,' said Ellen with savage satisfaction as they came out of school the afternoon before the great day. 'The sun rose red as red this morning.'

'But then you'll get wet when the Queen comes,' said Lucy Baines, wide-eyed. 'You're going too, you said you were.'

For the moment Ellen had forgotten all about her boastings. 'Oh, I shall be inside,' she said haughtily, 'not like you, standing out in the wet.'

'You'll be inside, locked in the pig-sty,' taunted Sarah Jarvis. 'Don't forget to see if the ladies have . . . legs,' she added daringly, and then ran away be-cause Miss Higgs was looking out of her window and might have heard her.

But when Ellen woke next morning and heard rain dripping from the gutter, from the porch, and pattering on the plants in the garden she did not feel glad at all. At that moment she would willingly have tossed away all her proud boastings and gone with the school to see the Queen, and the fact that it was a grey, soaking day only made her feel gloomier than ever. What was she going to do with herself? Everybody else had their plans, but she had a whole, dreary, wet day to fill all alone.

Her mother had no sympathy. 'No, you're certainly not going to be outside with me opening the gate for the Queen. If you're too naughty to go up with the school then you're certainly too naughty for that. Whatever would the Countess say ? You should have thought of all this before — it isn't as if I haven't told you till I'm tired. You'd better stay in the back and keep Moll and Martie quiet.'

But Ellen got tired of the four-year-old twins, who wanted to play by themselves, not with her. Sulkily she went out into the porch, and stared at the grey haze of rain that was sweeping over the park. There were footsteps coming down the road. She turned and saw Lucy and Mary Ann Baines, sheltering under a huge green umbrella.

'What are you doing, Ellen Timms ?' called Mary Ann. 'Waiting for the Queen ?'

'We're going to school,' said Lucy eagerly. 'To meet the others, and then we're all marching up that drive.' She pointed to the avenue beyond the gates.

37

'I was just setting out,' said Ellen
coolly. 'You'll get very wet, but I shall
be indoors.'

She reached for her mother's shawl
which hung by the door; Mam

wouldn't need it today, she would be wearing her Sunday one. Then she went down the path to the little garden gate, let herself out, and with a wary eye on the windows of the Lodge she opened the huge iron gates into the forbidden territory beyond. She didn't bother to close them, but turned and waved to the Baines sisters who were huddled under their umbrella, staring at her. Then she trotted on under the dripping trees.

She was alarmed at what she was doing, but she wasn't going back, not yet, anyway. The avenue went on and on in the shadow of the enormous beech trees. The rain pattered on the leaves overhead and splashed on to her in big cold drops, but she didn't care, she told herself; she was walking along the way the Queen was going to come.

Then the beech trees ended and she was out in the open. In front of her lay a huge house, as big as a whole village, with hundreds of windows in it and such a rolling carpet of grass in front and such flowerbeds. Ellen did come to a stop now, frightened by her own daring. There might be all sorts of people behind those windows, staring out at her. Even outside she could see plenty of people, running to and fro in the rain, between carts that stood on the gravel ahead of her and tents in the distance.

Any of the other village children would have run away, but Ellen had always had a bold nature to match her red hair. She was also very proud. If she turned back now she would have nothing to tell them at school; she would also probably run straight into

the whole school party headed by Miss
Higgs. So forward she marched.

In fact the people scurrying about on

the gravel and over the wet grass seemed far too busy to notice her. Ellen's courage picked up. She got quite close to the house, and stared up, marvelling. It was so high, you had to tip back your head to see the roof, and you could have fitted the Lodge in through any of the windows. She had ceased thinking about anybody stopping her, so she gave a violent start when a voice called to her.

'Who are you?' it said. It was a child's voice, but the sort of voice you obeyed.

Ellen jumped round. Quite near her stood a little girl in a tartan dress and a tartan cape with red hair escaping from under a green bonnet.

'Oh, now I know who you are,' said the little girl, 'because of your hair. You're the one who was so naughty when Mamma and I came to see your school. Well, I'm being naughty today. I'm tired of being told that I've got to be extra good because of the Queen. And we've had to move out of our nurseries so that the little princes' and princesses' nurses can go there. So I told Barley (that's our nurse) that I was going to be as naughty as I could. So I've run away into the rain. Is that what you're doing?'

Ellen looked at her feet and muttered yes, she had run away.

'Well, what naughty things shall we do?' said the little girl. 'I know, let's go and look inside those tents. Barley said she wasn't going to take us, so I'm being very disobedient and Barley would be very angry.'

Ellen was hardly listening to all this prattle. She was thinking with awe that here was one of The Family, and if she was with one of The Family then it wouldn't matter where she went — she might indeed even be able to look in through a window.

Nobody tried to stop them, nobody so much as glanced at them. They walked over wet lawns that squelched under their feet and soaked their shoes.

'Of course,' said the little girl reflectively, 'I'm being very naughty talking to you. I'm sure Barley wouldn't want me to, especially when you are so bad that they make you stand on a stool with a label. What's your name? My name is Mary. You can call me Lady Mary like Barley and the nursemaids do. Shall we go into this tent?'

The tent was as big as the whole school. It was funny to be inside, and yet walking

on grass. Rain drummed on the canvas
roof and there was a dim light and a
smell of trampled grass. There were
long, long tables spread with white cloths
and benches on either side of them.
People were hurrying up and down with
trays of glasses and plates and cutlery; but

nobody looked at the children. Ellen had never seen so many knives and forks in her life.

'Is this where the *Queen* is going to have her banquet?' she asked in an awed whisper.

'The Queen! Sitting on a bench in a tent!' said Lady Mary. 'How funny you are. This is where the village people are going to have their dinner of course. I wonder what they're going to eat. What do you eat at home?'

Ellen considered. 'We have the vegetables that Joe grows in the garden. And a bit of bacon. And pork when the pig's been killed. And pudding boiled in a cloth. Mam puts currants in it sometimes. They did say as how there was going to be roast beef and plum pudding today, and Johnnie (that's my brother) had a bet with Harry Price to see how many helpings they could get.'

'It sounds much nicer than what we have in the nursery. It's mutton most often, and rice pudding. And nobody's allowed to have more than one helping. But do you know what I've got here in my pocket? Lumps of sugar. I took them from Barley's cupboard. If we sat here under the table we could eat them without anybody seeing us.'

They sat on the damp grass with the tablecloth reaching down to the ground on either side and making a second tent all round them. Lady Mary put the lumps of sugar in two little piles. 'That's yours. Do you know, I don't think I've ever in my life been so naughty as I am today. Running away from Barley, talking to you, stealing sugar, and now sit-

ting on the grass. We're never, never
allowed to sit on the grass.'

'What do you sit on then?' asked
Ellen, puzzled.

'On chairs of course. Whatever do you
think? Barley says that people who sit on

grass catch their deaths. I don't know why.'

'But if you're outside what do you sit on?'

'We're always going for a walk if we're outside. Except on my birthday; that was last week. Then James (he's one of the footmen) brought out tea to the little garden house and we sat on little wooden benches and I poured out from my very own teapot. What do you think the best way of eating sugar is? Sucking it in your mouth or in your fingers? I like it in my fingers best, only it does fall to bits then. I do wish my pocket had been bigger and I had brought more.'

They sucked on noisily and in much content. Then Lady Mary crammed her hand over her mouth and giggled, pointing under the cloth.

'Isn't it funny to see people's feet when they can't see you! Wouldn't they be surprised if we just reached out and tickled them!'

Ellen looked at Lady Mary's little white-stockinged ankles creeping out from under her green and red and yellow dress. A question was wriggling about in her mind, but she was not sure whether she quite had the courage to bring it out.

'You know grown-up ladies,' she blurted out at last. 'Well, what I've wanted to know about is . . .'

'Yes?' said Lady Mary, staring at her.

'Is about their legs,' said Ellen with a rush. She was going to say a great deal more, all about her argument with the schoolchildren, but Lady Mary gave her no chance.

'You mustn't! It's wicked! Barley *never* allows us to say that. It's almost as bad as that other word we must never, never say. Shall I tell you what it is?' She looked all round very cautiously, as if there were spies even under the table, then shuffled close up to Ellen, put her mouth to her ear and whispered 'Stomach!' Her eyes opened wide at her daring. 'That's the wickedest thing I've done today,' she said with satisfaction. 'Now I think I'll go back to the house. I feel rather wet underneath me and perhaps I'm catching my death from sitting on the grass. There don't seem to be any feet; shall we go out now?'

They emerged on hands and knees into the vast canvas spaces.

'Plum pudding!' said Lady Mary longingly, looking at all the places laid

on the tables. 'Do you think if we stayed here we'd get a slice too? Still, I think I'd like to change my wet clothes first. Come on.'

Pulling Ellen behind her, she went out

into the open. There were many more people now, standing in groups and waiting in spite of the rain. And there Ellen saw some backs that she knew.

'It's the school,' she whispered pulling back, 'in their bonnets with the green ribbons that they bought special. And there's Miss Higgs. I dursen't go that way or Miss Higgs'll send me home.'

'Then you'd better come in the house with me. I tell you what, I'll show you where the Queen is going to have dinner tonight. It's the Picture Gallery, because the dining hall is too small. Look, we can go in this way.'

They crossed a vast stretch of gravel, with Ellen all the time expecting to hear Miss Higgs' sharp voice calling 'Ellen Timms, come here this instant.' Then they ran up a few steps and went in

through a glass-panel door. The door
shut behind them, and Ellen sighed with
relief. Miss Higgs hadn't seen her. The

stories she would be able to tell at school about having been inside the Great House!

Lady Mary was throwing her bonnet and her cape on the floor. 'Barley *would* be angry,' she said thoughtfully, looking at the crumpled heap. 'Now I'll take you to the Picture Gallery.'

She took Ellen's hand. They turned corners and climbed stairs and ran down long passages lined with doors. Then they stopped in front of one that had green baize nailed over it. Lady Mary slowly pushed it open, peeped round it fearfully and led the way through.

Ellen stood and gaped. It was all white and gold, and so huge – hundreds of times the size of Winterbourne Church, it seemed, and much lighter, because a lot of the roof was glass. And the pictures

of people — the size of real people — and the red carpet on the floor!

'The band's going to sit up here to

play music all through dinner. But you come here and see the tables.'

Lady Mary pulled Ellen over the red carpet. She found herself peering over carved railings down into a room far below. There were long tables spread with such sparkling silver and glass. There were silver candle holders and silver dishes and silver statues. You could hardly see the cloth, there was so much on the table. But it was the flowers she noticed most of all; flowers scattered on the table, standing in huge pots on the floor. She had never seen them indoors before.

'It's like a garden,' she quavered out loud.

'Ssh,' said Lady Mary, 'they'll hear you.'

There were all sorts of people

58

hurrying round down there, you could hear them murmuring like a hive of bees. 'Come and look into the hall. That's where the best flowers are.'

Ellen was dragged on again, over the carpet that felt as soft as mattresses to her feet.

'Here,' said Lady Mary, turning a corner. 'Look.'

Ellen gave a little shriek, because it was even bigger than the other place.

They were standing at the top of stairs that looked as though they had come out of a giant's palace. Twenty people could have marched down them abreast. They flowed like a white waterfall down to a hall so vast that Ellen's head swam, and on every step stood little trees in tubs. There were more in the hall, and

flowers and ferns too, and men in green and silver livery with white stockings and powdered hair.

Lady Mary pointed to doors in the

distance. Through glass panes you could catch a glimpse of grass far away. 'The Queen and the Prince and the little princes and princesses will come in through that door from their carriages. And Mamma and Papa will stand and welcome them. And then the Queen and her ladies will come up these stairs to the State Rooms to dress for luncheon. Then they'll go for a drive, then they'll look at some of the pictures, then lots of guests will come, then they'll all have dinner in the Picture Gallery.'

'Will you see them?' Ellen asked with awe. 'So as to speak to them?'

'I was going to,' said Lady Mary rather regretfully. 'We were all going to put on our best dresses and play with Princess Victoria and Prince Bertie and Princess Alice and Prince Alfred and show them our toys. But now Barley will put me in the dark closet. And I always scream if she does and it makes me sick. Unless I went back now and told her I was very sorry, and didn't tell her till afterwards how I took you round the house. Will you promise not to tell anybody ?'

'Yes,' said Ellen, staring round her and not really listening.

'Cross your heart and hope you'll die ? (One of our nursemaids taught me that, but Barley says it's bad.)'

'Cross my heart and hope I'll die,' gabbled Ellen, with her mind on the splendid sight below.

'Well then,' said Lady Mary with satisfaction, 'you had better go, and I'll find Barley and tell her that I'm good now. But mind – if you tell anybody what I've shown you, you'll die and go to Hell.'

Ellen came to her senses. 'But I want to see the Queen,' she said.

'Oh *you* can't see the Queen, Barley wouldn't like that at all.'

'But I *want* to.' Ellen's passion was rising.

'You mustn't say "I want," ' said Lady Mary, shocked. 'Barley doesn't let us. She says "want will have to be your master." And now look what you've done. They've heard us.'

At the bottom of the stairs, far away, people were looking at them and calling up, and the men with powdered heads and white stockings were hurrying to the doors.

'There's Papa and Mamma – the Queen must be here. And there's *Barley*

– now I *will* have to go to the dark closet. Oh quick, run!'

Lady Mary pulled Ellen behind her. Over the thick carpets they rushed, down corridors, past people who called to them. The panic got into Ellen and she took charge, though she had no idea where she was running.

'Stop,' panted Lady Mary. 'This is the Queen's part of the house. Nobody's allowed in here. The nursemaids said we'd have our heads cut off if we did.'

One of the doors ahead of them rattled and opened. With a squeak of terror Ellen plunged through a half open door beside her. There was a huge bed hung with crimson and gold and she flung herself at it and crawled underneath. The hangings fell back into place, and there she was in darkness, lying on the floor.

Then she gave a little shriek because there was a face peering in at her.

'Quick, make room for me,' said Lady Mary in a distracted voice. 'I didn't mean to be this naughty.' She was gasping and panting. 'They'll cut off our heads if they find us. Even Barley said that was what they did to people who offended the Queen. So what'll they do to people who hide under her bed? They'll probably torture us like the picture in that book I found in the library. Oh I do wish I'd never met you. No wonder they put you on a stool in your school.'

The two girls lay there, stiff and straight with fright. The floor seemed to press into Ellen's bones and the carpet pricked through her clothes. Voices spoke outside, feet moved over the carpet. A long long time went by. Then the door swished open, skirts rustled over towards them, there was a murmur of voices.

At first she was too frightened to hear what was being said. Then, with the voices almost above her head, she could not help it.

'Everything has been put in readiness for your Majesty in the next room,' said one.

'If you will just allow me to take your travelling dress, ma'am,' said another. 'Robinson, bring her Majesty's dressing robe.'

Nothing in Ellen's life had ever been so terrifying as this. What was more, she could actually see the people in the room – the bottom of their skirts, at any rate – because there was a tiny gap between the hangings and the carpet. And one of them was the Queen!

There was a great rustling of clothes, it seemed to go on for ever. And then, painfully turning her head because the carpet hurt her cheek beyond bearing,

Ellen saw . . . and plunged her face to the floor in horror. She didn't care any longer how uncomfortable she was: she was far too frightened for that. She crammed her hands over her ears so that she would be deaf as well as blind.

Then, at last, Lady Mary prodded her. 'They've gone into the next room.'

Ellen didn't wait. She crawled out, flung herself at the door and ran, she didn't know where. Suddenly, there she was at the top of the white waterfall of stairs, with the doors to the outside world in the distance. She made for that like a hunted animal. People shouted at her, made grabs at her; she hazily remembered dodging round the trees in their tubs to avoid them.

And then she was out in the fresh air with rain falling cool on her face. She

pelted down steps and crunched over gravel. There were plenty of people outside, but they were walking briskly with heads bent against the rain and took no notice of her.

'Why, it's Ellen Timms,' said somebody.

There were the Baines sisters, and Sarah Jarvis beside them, very wet, all three. Ellen stopped. Her face was on fire with running, and her chest felt as though it was going to burst.

'Where've you been?' they asked.

'We saw the Queen,' said Lucy. Her face was radiant.

'I've been in the Great House,' said Ellen as haughtily as she could for panting.

'Ooh the storyteller!' said Sarah Jarvis.

'What did you see?' asked little Lucy eagerly.

'I saw lots of things.' Ellen didn't know whether to start with the flowers or the red carpet or the men in their powdered hair. Then she remembered 'Cross your heart and hope you'll die.' 'But I can't tell you because it's a secret,' she said miserably.

'What did I say!' scoffed Sarah Jarvis. 'It's all stories, her and her boastings!'

'I tell you what,' flashed out Ellen, 'I've seen something that none of you could ever see in a thousand years, something that nobody else in England's seen. But I can't tell you, because it's . . . not polite.'

'You didn't see,' whispered Lucy very low, 'about their legs?'

But Ellen was walking away with a

74

flaming face, because very likely, she thought, she would be put in prison if anybody found out that she had seen the QUEEN'S LEGS.

'There she goes,' called out Sarah Jarvis. 'Storyteller Carroty Timms!'

And Ellen was never able to tell anybody what she had seen.

Catherine Storr

LUCY
LUCY RUNS AWAY

'I wish I was a boy,' said Lucy. 'Boys are stronger. They have bicycles and real fights. Boys have adventures.' When the boys in the neighbourhood refuse to let her join their gang, Lucy is even more determined to prove her bravery. 'I shall be a detective. I shall walk around and find some terrible crime going on. I am Lew the Fabulous Detective.' But no one was more surprised than Lucy when she caught a thief. This adventure is told in *Lucy*.

In *Lucy Runs Away* eager for further adventures Lucy decides to leave home when she turns eight. So with a satchel bulging and her savings in her pocket, she sets off to the seaside as the Mysterious Outlaw.

Perfect stories for seven-year-olds and upwards.